Disney's

Doug ™ Created by Jim Jinkins

The Funnie Mysteries

Jurassic Doug

by Kim Ostrow

Illustrated by Ray daSilva

Jurassic Doug is hand-illustrated by the same Grade A
Quality Jumbo artists who bring you
Disney's Doug, the television series.

DISNEY PRESS

New York

Original characters for "The Funnies" developed by
Jim Jinkins and Joe Aaron.

Printed in the United States of America

1 3 5 7 9 10 8 6 4 2

The artwork for this book was prepared using pen and ink.

The text for this book is set in 13-point Leewood.

Library of Congress Catalog Card Number: 00-108730

ISBN 0-7868-4458-2

For more Disney Press fun, visit www.disneybooks.com

CONTENTS

JURASSIC DOUG

Doug and Skeeter were standing by their lockers after school.

"Learning about archaeology is pretty cool," said Skeeter, as he skateboarded around Doug. "Wouldn't it be great to go on our own dig?"

"Yeah, man, let's do it!" Doug said. "How about this afternoon?"

"Can't. Spending some 'quality time' with my dad. My mom's making us mow the lawn together."

"Bummer. But you know what? I may just go on that dig myself," Doug said.

"Who knows what I could discover!"

"I discovered something incredible," Roger Klotz said loudly.

"Oh, yeah?" Doug replied.

"Yeah. I discovered what an incredible loser you are." His gang cackled behind him as they all turned and left.

Just then, Patti Mayonnaise showed up. She had been watching from her locker.

"Don't pay any attention to him, Doug," she said sweetly. "I think going on a dig would be great."

"Uh . . . thanks, Patti," Doug said, blushing. He thought she was the prettiest, smartest girl in the whole world.

"Let me know what you come up with," Patti said as she was leaving.

Skeeter wished Doug the best of luck, and Doug hurried home.

The archaeological dig was about to begin. As Doug came out of the garage with his shovel, Porkchop was standing in front of him with a gift.

"For me?" Doug asked.

Porkchop nodded as he handed Doug his present.

"I guess every archaeologist needs one of these," Doug said, placing the funny-looking hat on his head. It had a light in the front and a fan in the back for ventilation.

"Thanks, Porkchop! Wish you could skip your Sculpting for Doggies class and help me dig," Doug said. Porkchop

nodded, heading off in his artist's smock. "See you when I discover something big!" Doug yelled after him.

And with that, Doug was off to find the perfect place to start his excavation.

After a few hours of digging in his backyard, Doug was feeling tired, hot, and a bit less certain about finding an ancient artifact. But every time he was about to stop, he remembered how Roger had laughed at him; and so Doug kept going. Suddenly, his shovel hit something.

"Wow!" Doug shouted from the bottom of the hole. "What is this?"

Excited, he climbed out with his newest discovery. Dusting it off, he couldn't believe what he saw.

"This looks like some kind of fossilized

footprint!" Doug said to himself. "It looks *really* old. Maybe it's a dinosaur impression like the ones we studied! I'd better go look it up in my dinosaur book."

In his room, Doug flipped through his entire collection of dinosaur books, hoping to match his discovery. But no matter how many books, he looked in, Doug couldn't match the print. He wondered what it could be . . . maybe some entirely new, undiscovered dinosaur!

As Doug hugged his fossil, his imagination took over. There he stood, in front of thousands of television cameras and reporters. Everyone wanted to get a look at Doug and the amazing Dougasaurus footprint.

"Oh, Doug," said Patti, who was standing by his side on the steps of the museum. "After this, I bet they're going to change the expression from 'archaeological dig' to 'archaeological Doug'!"

When the fossil was unveiled, cameras flashed all around Doug. After all, it was the greatest discovery since Banana Pizza!

"Mr. Funnie!" shouted a reporter as he shoved his microphone near Doug's face. "Tell us again what this is! And how you found it. And where'd you get that cool hat?"

"Well, it's a funny story, actually. . . ."

Doug began. The entire crowd burst out laughing.

"Oh, Doug," said Patti. "You're so . . . archaeologist-y!"

She leaned in to give him a kiss. But all Doug felt was slurping.

"Wha—? Oh, Porkchop," said Doug, back in the real world. "Did you see what I found?"

When Porkchop saw what Doug was holding, his eyes opened wide. He looked as surprised as Doug. But before he could even growl, Judy swooped in and scooped up Porkchop.

"Sorry, little brother," she said. "I need to borrow your canine companion for my 'Gathering of Quadrupeds' performance piece."

And with that, she dragged him away. As they disappeared, Doug heard Judy say, "Porchop, walk on all fours! You're no good to me on two feet! Why can't you be more like a real dog?"

"Aw, man!" Doug complained out loud. "I wanted to know what Porchop thinks about my latest discovery! Oh, well," he said to himself. "I'd better get ready to take my discovery to the museum. They're going to flip when they see what I have."

Doug went to his closet to find his best outfit. Since he was going to be on everyone's TV set in a matter of hours, he wanted to look nice. Doug took his time picking something nice to wear

Carefully wrapping up the fossil and

hiding it under his shirt, Doug headed for the museum.

A few minutes into his walk, he encountered an obstacle.

"Where are you going, Doug?" said the obstacle.

It was Beebe Bluff.

"Uh . . . nowhere?" he replied, thinking quickly.

Beebe was staring at Doug's stomach. She was thinking that maybe Doug had made too many trips to Swirly's this week.

"What have you been eating lately?" Beebe asked, looking at Doug's bulging stomach. "Or should I ask what *haven't* you been eating lately?" She poked him in the stomach.

"Hey! What's under there?" she asked suspiciously.

"Um . . . nothing?" Doug said.

"Well, it looks like a pretty big nothing to me!" Beebe said. "What is it? Why are you hiding it under your shirt? You're up to something and I want to know what it is! How many vanilla shakes will it take for you to tell me? I have to know!"

Doug needed to do some fast thinking. He wanted the museum people to be the first viewers. Just then, he saw a strange little kid sailing down the block on a scooter. As the kid got closer, Doug realized that he knew him. It was Porkchop, and he looked worried.

"Hey, Porkchop," Doug said. And before Beebe could say another word, Doug was swooped up off the sidewalk and onto the scooter.

"Wow, you're sure in a hurry to get me to the museum," Doug said as Porkchop handed him a helmet. "Good idea, taking this scooter. We'll be across town in no time flat!"

Porkchop was making all kinds of

noise. Doug was flattered that his best buddy was so excited for him. All of a sudden, Porkchop turned the scooter and headed toward home.

"Hey!" Doug said. "This isn't the way to the museum. No one will see my discovery if we keep it hidden!" Doug jumped off the scooter—just missing a muddy puddle.

Porkchop stopped the scooter and began frantically gesturing at Doug.

"Oh! I see," said Doug. "I get it now."

Porkchop was happy that Doug finally realized what was going on.

"I get it, old pal," Doug said to his trusty friend. "I see why you've kidnapped me, and diverted me from where I was going. I even know why you're acting so funny."

"Roo-oow?" Porkchop replied hopefully.

"I guess with all my digging and your sculpting classes, we haven't spent much time together," Doug said. "Well, let's just fix that right now!"

Porkchop shook his head.

"I know it can get lonely sometimes. But fame and fortune have waited twelve and a half years already, so, what's a little more time? The museum can wait," Doug announced.

He carefully placed his fossilized clay print on the ground. It was time to play with Porkchop. However, all Porkchop wanted to do was get near the print.

"Careful, Porkchop. I'm just putting fame on hold for a little while. Maybe you shouldn't get so close to the fossil. If we break it, I might let down the museum."

Porkchop sighed heavily.

"C'mon," Doug said. "Let's hang out over here. *Away* from the print!"

Porkchop headed toward his friend, dragging his paws a bit as he walked through a muddy puddle.

As Doug watched his pal pad toward him, he finally figured everything out!

Doug followed Porkchop's muddy prints along the sidewalk.

Doug looked at the prints from Porkchop's four paws. Then he looked at the huge, single print captured in clay. The truth hit him like a ton of fossilized clay paw impressions.

Doug placed the clay fossil in front of Porkchop.

With a smile, Porkchop balanced himself carefully until his paws fit into the clay.

"Just as I suspected!" Doug shouted. "Your paws are a perfect match!" Doug had not found one large paw print; he had found four smaller ones.

Porkchop nodded. Finally, Doug understood!

Porkchop explained that the prints were part of an art project he had been working on. Some of his earlier work. But, being the perfectionist that he was, when the art didn't turn out exactly as he wanted, he had buried it in the backyard.

"So picking me up on that scooter and taking me home was all part of a bigger plan?" Doug asked.

"Rrrrrrow!"

"And all that frantic paw waving wasn't for attention, huh?"

Porkchop nodded.

"Wow, thanks, Porkchop," Doug said. "You sure saved me from an embarrassing situation! I guess I didn't find a Dougasaurus, I found a Dogasaurus!"

The two headed home. This time it was

Doug who drove the scooter. "Well, fame will just have to wait a few more years . . . unless . . . Porkchop, what else do you have buried in the backyard?"

Porkchop barked, but Doug just laughed. "Just kidding," he said. "I think I've had enough archaeology for a while!"

DOGGONE DAYS

Doug was at Swirly's, sadly sipping a Chocolate Frothy Goat. He sighed as he twirled the straw around and around. When Patti Mayonnaise came in, she couldn't help noticing Doug's gloomy mood.

"Hey, Doug," Patti said, smiling. "What's the matter?"

Normally, Patti's presence would have perked Doug right up. But today, he had other things on his mind.

"It's Porkchop," said Doug.

"Porkchop? Is he okay?" Patti asked, concerned.

"How would I know?" Doug replied glumly.

Just then, Skeeter made his way into Swirly's. He had his skateboard under his arm.

"What's wrong, man? You look bummed out," Skeeter said.

"I don't think Porkchop wants to be my friend anymore," said Doug.

"What?" Skeeter said. "C'mon, man! Porkchop is your best friend. Well, your best nonhuman friend. What are you talking about?"

"It all started on Monday. I came home at my usual time. Hungry from a long day at school, I was ready to share some milk and cookies with Porkchop."

"Sounds cool," Skeeter said.

"Well, that's what I thought. But when I got home, Porkchop was nowhere to be found! He finally showed up hours later and didn't want any part of his milk and cookies. He went straight to his tepee."

Skeeter and Patti looked worried. "No cookies? That's not like Porkchop!" said Skeeter.

"Yeah, I know," Doug continued. "And every day since then has been exactly the same! Home from school: no Porkchop."

"Hmmmm," said Patti. "That sounds awfully mysterious."

Doug thought about it. He nodded. He thought Patti was as right as a plate of Tater Twisties for two.

"I've got some stuff to do," Doug said, getting up from the booth. "I'll talk to you later. Oh, and thanks for your help!"

Patti and Skeeter didn't quite know what they had done, but they were always happy to help their friend.

Doug ran all the way home. I've got to get to the bottom of this, he thought. Patti had made him realize that this wasn't a Porkchop problem—it was a Porkchop mystery!

When Doug finally got home, he ran to his room to find his detective notebook. As he put a pencil behind his ear, he headed for Porkchop's tepee to look for clues.

"Clue number one," Doug said out loud as he scribbled in his notebook. "Missing person . . . oh, wait, scratch that . . . missing dog from backyard tepee; usually meets best human friend after school. Very suspicious."

Doug looked around the lawn for any other suspicious matter. There was a large sculpture of something vaguely resembling the lunch special at the school cafeteria.

Before Doug could investigate further, a loud noise shrieked in his ear. "Doug Funnie!" said the noise.

It was his sister, Judy. There was clay all over her face.

"Is this a larger-than-life-size sculpture of Turkey Surprise?" Doug asked her, chuckling. He knew Judy had to be working on another art project for The Moody School for the Gifted.

"Oh, Dougie, your mind is so . . . small. You wouldn't know fine art if it fell on your head. It happens to be an abstract sculpture of *La Femme Judy*." She gestured to herself and bowed dramatically.

"Well, you're right about one thing. It's abstract!" Doug replied.

"Get out of my art studio!" she bellowed.

"This is our backyard," Doug said as he continued to patrol the area.

"Have you no vision! How can an artist be expected to create beauty with all these humdrum distractions? And get that mongrel away from my clay!"

Mongrel?

Doug spun around and came face-to-face with the subject of his investigation.

"Porkchop!" Doug shouted happily as he hugged his long-lost friend.

"Rrrr-row?" Porkchop answered. He sagged limply as Doug hugged him, and then quickly disappeared into his tepee.

"What's the matter, Porkchop?" Doug said through the tepee flap.

Doug heard something that sounded like snores.

"Tired?"

But there was no answer.

"How about a snack?" Doug asked. "Mr. Swirly has a Peanutty Buddy with your name written all over it!"

But Porkchop didn't seem interested in his favorite snack. The only response Doug could detect from the tepee was louder snores.

Dejected, Doug went to his room to study his clues. Lying on his bed, he opened the notebook and wrote, "Clue 1, subject follows unusual behavior patterns. Clue 2, subject refuses favorite snack." This felt like the hardest case Doug had ever come up against. What had happened to his best friend?

The next morning seemed like it was going to be a much better day. After all, it was Saturday, and Doug had all day to solve his mystery. Doug wanted a head start, so he got up early and crept downstairs. He opened the door and headed toward Porkchop's tepee.

"Rise and shine, Porkchop," Doug sang outside the tepee. "Time for breakfast! How about a little trip to Suicide Mountain

Skateboard Park to watch Skeeter try out some new moves?"

Doug waited a moment. Maybe Porkchop was in the shower.

Doug waited and waited and waited. Nothing happened. He peeked in the tepee—but Porkchop was gone!

Doug immediately took out the notebook and wrote down his new information.

I'm going to get to the bottom of this, he thought, trying to keep his spirits up.

Just then, Doug's dad made his way outside.

"Big Funnie barbecue this afternoon, pal," said Phil Funnie. "Would you mind getting my chef's hat from the garage while I fire up the ol' grill?"

"Sure, Dad," said a downhearted Doug.

"That's my boy!"

Doug walked over to the garage. He put his detective notebook back in his pocket. It's no use, he thought, Porkchop just doesn't want to be my best friend anymore.

Entering the garage, Doug looked for the chef's hat. It wasn't in its usual spot. He looked everywhere, but it wasn't in the garage.

Hmmmm, could this be a clue? Doug wondered.

Just then, he spotted something out of the corner of his eye: a strange figure running past him dressed in a colorful outfit.

"Hey," Doug said. "That's Dad's chef's

hat! And Judy's cos-
tume for her spring
opera, *P Stands for
Pasta*!"

Inspired once again,
Doug whipped out his
notebook and wrote
down his newest clue.
He knew it was only
a matter of time
before he solved this
mystery.

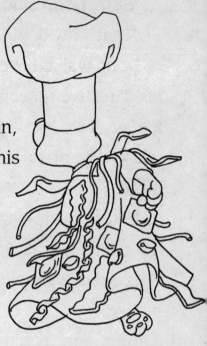

Later that day, Doug was helping his dad
with the barbecue. While he watched Phil
try to get the coals lit, Doug noticed a
commotion coming from Porkchop's
tepee.

"I'll be right back," Doug said to his dad.

Slowly, Doug made his way over to the tepee. A familiar smell tickled his nose. This tepee smells like Mom in the kitchen on lasagna day, Doug thought.

And with that, Porkchop came out of his tepee. The two stared at each other. Porkchop looked a bit sad. Then he ran to Doug, hugged him, and ran off again.

"Wait!" shouted Doug. And speaking of weight, Doug noticed that Porkchop had gained some. He was looking a little portly.

What is going on? Doug wondered. I must solve this mystery before it's too late.

But was it already too late?

Doug looked over his clues.

1) Porkchop's change of routine
2) Refusal of favorite snack
3) A strange figure running around in Dad's chef's hat and Judy's old costume
4) Porkchop's tepee smelling like lasagna
5) Porkchop looking chubby

Doug paced in his room, trying to figure things out. And then, while staring at a poster of his favorite actor, Daniel Dravot, he had an idea. He remembered that for his last role, Daniel Dravot had gained a lot of weight to make his character more believable.

Now Doug knew what was wrong with Porkchop.

Porkchop was leaving Doug to pursue a life in acting. Now, it all made sense. He was never around because he was rehearsing. He was on a strict diet of lasagna to make him gain weight. He was borrowing costumes to get into character. Another mystery solved! Doug had done it again! Happy for a few minutes at his discovery and excellent sleuthing skills, Doug went to get a snack. But on the way to the kitchen a new thought struck him.

"If Porkchop has left me to become an actor," Doug said to himself, "then he's not going to be around to be my best friend anymore!"

This was the worst news Doug had heard all year. Doug was back to where he started—downhearted and dogless.

Just then, that same almost-lasagna smell wafted under his nose. He sniffed, following the aroma. He followed it all the way to his neighbor's backyard!

There stood Mr. Dink with a chef's hat on. And right next to him was Doug's long-lost pal!

"Porkchop?" said Doug quizzically.

"Douglas, my boy!" shouted a happy Mr. Dink. "Do come over! Welcome to *Chez Pooch*!"

"Huh?" answered Doug, confused.

"I hope you don't mind my borrowing your little friend here. I started a little business venture and it wasn't going so well. I thought Porkchop might know what the dogs of today want in their eating establishments."

Doug looked at Porkchop, who didn't look so little anymore!

"He's been helping me run this new Italian restaurant for dogs. Bone Pizza is our specialty!"

"Rrro-ow!" said a proud Porkchop.

"This little guy can sure cook up a

mean pizza!" said Mr. Dink, pointing at Porkchop.

"So that's why Porkchop has been missing so much! And been so tired and full! And smelled like tomato sauce! And why he's wearing Judy's pasta robe!"

Doug was relieved that Porkchop hadn't caught the acting bug.

But Doug still had one more job to do before this mystery was over.

Sitting down at a table with Porkchop and Mr. Dink, Doug explained, "I think it's great that you wanted to open a restaurant for the dogs of the neighborhood. And the smells are delicious. But you know what dogs of today want?"

Mr. Dink leaned in closer.

"They just want pals to hang around

with. And a few treats from time to time."

"I see, Douglas. Well, if that's the case, perhaps I can just work on creating some bone pizza treats for dogs. Because as I always say, nothing adventured, nothing gained."

Porkchop and Doug looked at each other. And then nodded, of course.

"And I've missed having you around!" Doug told Porkchop. "How about you throw in your chef's hat and come back as my best friend?"

"Rrrrrro-oooow!"

The two best friends were back in business.

And Mr. Dink had a new business of his own. And a good canine consultant in the tepee next door!

"How about a Peanutty Buddy?" Doug suggested as they walked home arm in arm.

Porkchop patted his little plump belly.

"Maybe later!" Doug said. "Way later!"

The two laughed all the way home.

CARTOON CAPER

It was a sunny day in Bluffington. Doug and Porkchop were sitting on the grass in the backyard, reading *The Bluffington Gazette*. Porkchop was reading the business section. Doug was checking out what was happening around town.

"Hey, Porkchop, look at this!" Doug said excitedly, pointing to the newspaper. Porkchop put down his section.

"Looks like there's going to be a contest in Bluffington," Doug said. "It's a contest with clues—my specialty!"

The announcement read:

> Beware! Monster Bars are coming to Bluffington!
>
> A lifetime supply may just crash on your doorstep if you can find me!
>
> Look for clues in my upcoming cartoons.
>
> Signed,
> Munching Monster

Doug was up for the challenge. After all, who solved more mysteries than he did? And he was a master of cartoons. He was a sure bet to win a lifetime supply of Monster Bars. Whatever they were!

The fine print at the bottom of the page said that for the next few days there would be a clue hidden in each cartoon—

including a clue as to where in Bluffington the Munching Monster would be. Whoever was the first to figure out all the clues would win a year's supply of Monster Bars.

"Let the games begin, Porkchop," Doug said, tapping his detective notebook.

The next day in school, everyone had a copy of the morning newspaper.

"Face it, Funnie," said Roger, clutching a copy of the paper. "I'm going to enjoy a year's worth of candy. So you and your loser friends can just give up now."

Doug ignored Roger and went on with his day. Every chance he got he opened the newspaper and looked at the day's cartoon. The cartoon was of a big monster footprint with strange writing inside it.

YAWRUOYNOERAUOY

Doug sighed. The monster spoke a language no one had ever heard before! How was he going to find out where this monster was if he couldn't decipher what the monster was saying?

Doug stared at the paper and scratched his head. Then he wrote down the clue in his notebook. Even though he had no clue what it meant! This was harder than he had expected. He tried unscrambling the letters. But all he came up with was YAWN YOUR YEAR . . . with OUO left over. No, that couldn't be it!

Roger interrupted his thinking.

"Hey, Funnie," he said. "Even a loser like you should know I'm going to figure out this contest before you do!"

And off Roger went, laughing out loud.

Doug walked home from school, trying to understand the clue.

The next morning, Doug rushed to see the morning paper. He couldn't wait for another clue.

This time, there were no words. Only a picture of the monster holding a bad-minton birdie.

Doug wrote down his second clue.

"Hmmm," he said. "I wonder what a birdie has to do with anything."

Doug looked over his clues. "Let's see," he said to himself. "First we have a message in some monster language. Then a piece of sporting equipment. Very interesting."

"Who are you talking to, oh pathetic, uncultured brother of mine?" asked Judy. She was wearing flippers and a snorkel mask.

"Why are you dressed like a fish?"

"The Punt 'n' Grunt donated them to our school. So as a drama assignment, I'm living the rest of the day as a fish," she said, flopping her fins. "Now, do you mind? You're polluting my ocean."

And then the second clue began to make sense. Judy's mentioning the store made Doug think of the birdie the monster was holding. That made him realize that the monster would be appearing at the Punt 'n' Grunt. Now if only he could understand the monster's language. . . .

The next morning's paper brought the

third and final clue. This was Doug's last chance to figure out the mystery. He flipped through the pages of the newspaper until he found the cartoon.

"Aw, man!" Doug said to himself when he saw it. "It's in that strange language again!"

The cartoon showed a furry monster hand holding an invitation.

RENNIWEHTERAUOY

A note below the cartoon said:

Taking out his detective notebook, Doug wrote down the lucky phrase. He wrote it right next to the other one.

YAWRUOYNOERAUOY

RENNIWEHTERAUOY

He took the words apart and put them back together. He came up with lots of different words: NO, WAR, AHOY, WHERE, THEIR, RAY, RAT, RUNWAY, WIENER . . . But none of them seemed like the answer. He decided to walk around the neighborhood for inspiration.

Doug took his notebook so he could walk and think about the clues at the same time. He walked around for a long time. But he couldn't come up with a thing. This wasn't like him. He always solved the case!

Doug consoled himself. He knew that all good mysteries were solved in good time. And with good snacks. So he called Skeeter and Patti and asked them to meet him at Swirly's for more thinking—and ice cream. As he waited for his friends to arrive, Doug slurped his Chocolate Frothy Goat and imagined himself winning the contest. He sat atop a mountain of Monster Bars. Patti was right by his side.

"How on earth did you ever figure out this mystery?" Patti asked him.

"Well, Patti," Doug recounted, "it was very complicated."

"Oh, Doug," she said, admiringly. "You are so mysterious!"

Doug was popped out of his imagination by the sound of his slurping! Just then, Skeeter and Patti popped in the door of Swirly's.

"Hey, man," Skeeter said as he slid into the booth. "Did you get the answer to the contest yet?"

"Hey, guys," Doug said. "I haven't figured it out yet—but I'm not giving up until I do."

"You're a very determined detective, Doug," said Patti.

Doug blushed.

"Just as determined as Guy Graham," she continued. "He showed me a list of a hundred words he had made from the letters in the monster's clues."

The color in Doug's cheeks turned from red to green. He couldn't understand what Patti saw in a guy who was always staring at himself in the mirror. Doug picked up his super-size Swirly spoon, and caught his own reflection in it. And suddenly the answer was staring him in the face.

"Thanks to you guys," Doug said, jumping up, "I'm going to solve this contest once and for all!"

"See ya, man," said Skeeter.

But Doug was already out the door. As the door to Swirly's shut behind him, he checked out his reflection in the glass door.

"Woo-hoo!" he shouted when he saw himself. "I'm going to win! I'm going to win!"

Doug knew he had to get home as soon as possible. He had to fill out the contest form, and be back at the store with the magic phrase. He was running as fast as he could when he literally bumped into his neighbor, Mr. Dink.

"Hey! Slow down there, Douglas," he said. "What's the big hurry?"

"I'm about to win a contest!" Doug shouted. "But I have to get home to fill out the entry form!"

"All right, my boy," Mr. Dink started. "But as someone who has won many a contest in his day, remember this. The contest isn't over until the grass is greener on the other side of the fence."

Doug scratched his head.

"I'll remember that!" Doug said as he

started running. "See ya!"

And with that, Doug was off and running again.

Mr. Dink sighed and smiled. "Ah, youth."

When Doug got home he ran to his room.

"Porkchop, I figured it out! The clues were all spelled backward! I saw them when I looked at my reflection in the door at Swirly's! Look!"

"Rrro-oow!"

"Not only have I solved the case, but I'm about to win the contest. C'mon!"

Doug quickly filled out his entry. Then he grabbed Porkchop and they ran back to the Punt 'n' Grunt. There were lots of people there. Doug wondered if everyone else

had figured out the clues, too. Doug went to stand with Patti and Skeeter. Roger and his gang were taking up the whole front row.

"Hey, Funnie," he called. "You know what's funny? The fact that a loser like you thinks he could ever win this contest!"

All of the sudden, a huge furry monster entered the store. Everyone gasped.

"Welcome to the Monster Bar Contest!" a voice shouted. "Please welcome the Munching Monster!"

The crowd applauded.

An announcer was on a little stage, welcoming the monster.

"Thank you all for coming," he said.

"I know the winning phrase!" shouted

Roger. "I unscrambled the letters." He had already jumped up on the stage to collect his prize. He tossed his entry at the announcer.

"All right, young man," said the announcer. "What's the correct answer?"

Roger opened his mouth as wide as he could and blurted out, "Ahoy there, Rine!" he said confidently. "Can I have my Monster Bars NOW?"

Everyone started whispering.

"What does *rine* mean?" Skeeter whispered to Doug.

"It means he lost the contest!"

Roger was busy patting himself on the back when the announcer said, "I'm sorry, that is incorrect."

"Is the answer 'No Way, Wiener'?"

called out Guy Graham. "Or 'Where Are You, Ray'?"

"No, no," said the announcer.

"Um . . . I know the answer," Doug called from the back of the room.

He was asked to come right up.

Feeling a little nervous, Doug walked up on stage. But when he saw Patti's face, he had all the confidence of Smash Adams. He handed his entry to the announcer.

"What's your name, young man?"

"Doofus Doug," shouted Roger.

"My name is Doug Funnie," Doug said proudly, "and I figured it out."

Everyone listened.

"The winning phrase is . . . 'You Are The Winner,'" Doug said.

The announcer smiled. "Doug, YOU are the winner," he said. Balloons were released. Streamers flew through the air. Music started trumpeting.

"Doug Funnie is the winner!"

The whole store cheered!

Doug decided to have a party at Swirly's. After all, a lifetime of Monster Bars was great. But it was even better to have a roomful of friends to share them with.

He sat happily in his favorite booth. Patti and Skeeter sat on one side. The monster sat on the other. As they sipped their Frothy Goats, the monster took out a pen and wrote a message in Doug's detective notebook. It said,

EZIRPTSEBEHTERASDNEIRF

MYSTERY NOTES

The snow was coming down pretty hard outside Doug Funnie's window.

"Looks like it's snowing Swirly's Vanilla Shakes out there," Doug said to his best nonhuman friend, Porkchop.

"Slurp," Porkchop agreed hungrily.

They sat on the floor together, looking through a stack of comic books. Doug had stopped at the back of one of them and was looking at an ad for the Smash Adams Super Spy Investigator's Kit.

"I wonder if my investigator's kit will

come today," said Doug. "I sent for it two weeks ago. Feels like it'll never get here."

Porkchop shrugged and made an "I don't know" sound.

Doug stared outside as the wind blew snow all over the place. He wondered if there would even be mail today.

"Let's go check the mailbox, Porkchop," Doug said, with his nose pressed up to the glass.

They ran downstairs.

"If you're getting the mail, Douglas, be sure to wear a scarf, hat, boots, gloves, and a coat," Doug's mom called from the kitchen. "It's cold out there."

Then Doug's sister Judy appeared at the top of the stairs. *"Excusez moi,"* she sang loudly.

Doug looked up. Judy was wearing her favorite beret and a feather boa.

"Uh, what did you say?" Doug asked.

Judy said some more things Doug didn't understand.

"Your sister is doing a whole play in French," said Theda Funnie. "The director said that she needs to eat, sleep, and breathe French. For the next few days, your sister isn't allowed to say anything in English!"

Judy walked down the stairs dramatically with a big French book under her arm.

"Pardonez moi," she said, rolling her eyes at Doug.

Doug and Porkchop just stood there, mouths open, looking at her.

"Zat means get out of my way, Monsieur Pathétique and his oh-so-un-French-poodle-like doggie," she snapped, moving the two of them aside.

"I thought you couldn't say anything in English," Doug said to his sister. "Using a bad French accent isn't the same as speaking French!"

Judy ignored him and went to make french fries.

Anxious to see if his investigator's kit had arrived, Doug and Porkchop walked into the winter wonderland. Doug dusted the snow off the mailbox and opened it.

"Hey," Doug's voice echoed inside the mailbox. "Look at this!"

He pulled out a big envelope addressed to him. 'TOP SECRET' was stamped on the

front. Excited, Doug ripped opened the letter. It said:

> What is the first thing you should do?
> Search your driveway for a clue.

Never one to pass up a mystery, Doug was on the case. He wasn't sure if this was his mystery-solving kit, but he sure was curious! Up and down the driveway, the two looked around to find a clue. Unfortunately, snowdrifts a foot high were covering the driveway. Even though it had finally stopped snowing, Doug still couldn't see anything that looked like a clue.

"Man, it couldn't have snowed at a worse time for me!" he said.

Sitting on a small hill of snow, Doug tried to come up with a plan. "Guess I'll have to shovel this driveway, Porkchop, if I want to find this clue."

It was cold on Jumbo Street as Doug shoveled. He thought about summer vacation to stay warm.

Lifting the last shovelful of snow off the driveway, Doug's shovel scraped up against a metal box. Doug opened the small box. Hidden inside was another note. It said:

> Something is coming in this snowy weather.
>
> Your clue will be found when you put it together.

"At least we can wait inside," Doug said thankfully.

Just then, Doug's neighbor Mr. Dink walked up.

"What are you doing, Douglas, my boy?" asked Mr. Dink.

"Just trying to solve a mystery," Doug answered.

"Ahhh . . . mysteries," said Mr. Dink dreamily. "They're so . . . mysterious! As I always say, Douglas, never solve a mystery if it ain't broke."

Doug scratched his head.

"Oh, by the way, this came to my house by mistake," Mr. Dink said, handing over a large box. "Good luck with your mystery. I'm off to Raccoon Records to buy that new *Clogging to the Classics* record. The wife wants us to take up clogging, and I want to get a head start before the class begins. Pretty groovy, right, Douglas?"

"Uh . . . sure, Mr. Dink. Have fun! And thanks for the package."

Porkchop had jumped on top of the box and was checking its dimensions with a tape measure.

"This must be our second clue, Porkchop," Doug said confidently. "Let's go open it!"

Inside his room, Doug struggled with

the box. An instruction sheet fell out. Looking at the picture, Doug thought it would be no problem to assemble. With a little help from Porkchop, of course. Porkchop appeared with a tool belt and some protective eyewear.

"Rrrrr-row!" said Porkchop.

And with that, they began putting their clue together.

"There sure are a lot of pieces and wires here," Doug said, worried.

They put pieces together. And then took them apart! They put slot A into slot B. Then retried it putting slot C into slot D.

How did I get into this mess? wondered

Doug. But in the name of good detecting they tried one last time.

"Aha!" Doug said.

Porkchop and Doug stared hard at their work.

"What is it?" Doug asked.

"Rrrr-ow?"

"Seems to be some sort of toaster! And look!" Doug said as he pulled out a tiny envelope stuck to the bottom of the toaster. It said:

> In order to solve this really hard mystery
>
> Pay close attention to your little sister-y!

"My sister?" Doug said suspiciously. "How could she lead me to my Smash Adams kit?"

But Doug had come too far to give up now. So off to the living room he went to watch Cleopatra Dirtbike, his little sister, and see if she could lead him to another clue.

Doug watched her gurgle and play in the living room. He followed her closely as she scooted around and happily chewed on her toy moose. Then he moved in as she made some music with a few pots and pans. Doug watched carefully, but wondered how Dirtbike would lead him to his next clue. He wondered if Smash Adams had a sister who was the key to solving some of the great spy mysteries of his time. I doubt it, Doug said to himself with a sigh. And then his mind wandered. And in no time, Doug Funnie was transformed into Smash Adams, Ultrasuave Spy.

"I'm so suave," said Smash Adams. "I can spy on anyone. And they'll never suspect me. Because I'm suave."

Smash Adams was on The Case of the Missing Big Sister. He suavely had to spy on his family and see if he could locate his sister. Who was missing. He surveyed his living room with special binoculars hidden in his shoes. All around the house Smash dashed, spying on its inhabitants. He spied on his mother making hot chocolate. He spied on his father working on some new and improved spy cameras for Smash to use on other spy cases.

"Good work, Dad," Smash whispered.

And then, hot on the trail of his missing sister, he came upon the door to her room.

"Perhaps my missing sister is in her

room," said Smash.

He spied through the keyhole and spotted her on the phone. She was surrounded by some mysterious cleaning products. Just then, her eye caught Smash's eye.

"Doog Fooneeee!" Judy screeched in a French accent. "Am-scray!"

Doug popped out of his fantasy and ran downstairs. There Dirtbike was chewing on a familiar-looking envelope.

He opened it and read his newest clue. It said:

> Your next-to-last clue will be oh-so-easy to see
> When the bathtub reflects the face of Doug Funnie.

"No way!" Doug shouted. "Not in this lifetime!" He knew who was sending the mystery notes and why.

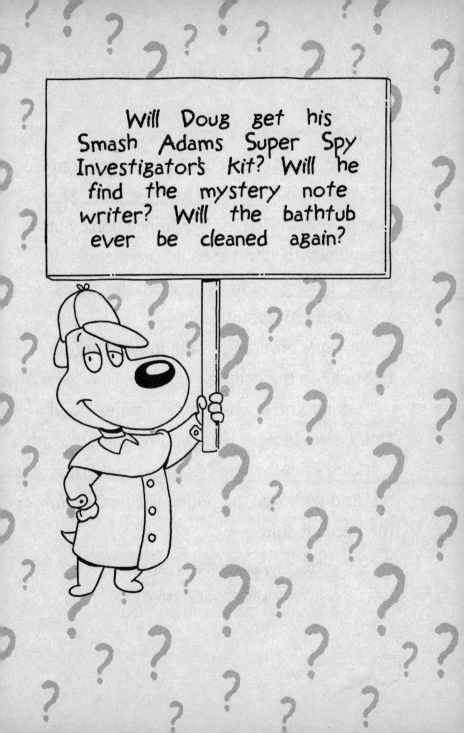

Up the stairs Doug flew. He knocked on Judy's door.

"Judy n'est pas ici!" said Judy.

"Aha!" Doug cried, bursting in to her room.

"Aha?" said Judy in a funny accent. She was pretending to read her French book, but Doug knew better. He could see a sheet of paper sticking out from between the pages.

"I knew it!" Doug said.

"Je parle français," said Judy, pointing her nose to the ceiling.

"I don't know what you're saying," said Doug. "But I know what you're doing!"

Doug knew where his final clue would be. And with that, he pulled the note from the book. It said:

> This mystery will end very soon
> If you clean up Judy's room!

"You've been making me do all your chores today!" said a tired Doug.

"Je ne sais pas blah blah blah . . ." Judy pretended to not understand English.

Doug had solved many mysteries in his day, but he had never come up against a mind so deviously criminal as that of his sister. She had passed off her shoveling and baby-sitting chores on Doug by pretending they were part of a mystery. And she had gotten him and Porkchop to put together her toaster oven—her French toast–er oven—for her, too. "I can't believe you, Judy," said Doug.

"Moi?" Judy said, pointing to herself.

Just then, Doug's mom poked her head in Judy's room.

"I have been watching you all day, Douglas," said Theda. "I think it's just fantastic the way you've been helping Judy out, dear. You helped her with the shoveling and put together her French toast maker. You even helped with the baby. It just warms my heart to see my children work together!"

"But Mom, she's—" Doug protested.

"Mais, oui, Maman," said Judy, cutting him off smugly. *"Mon petit frère* has grown so much as a person. He's much more centered these days."

"Well," said Theda. "Since Doug has been such a help, I think we should all go out to dinner to celebrate. Maybe for French food."

Doug had had enough of French things for one day. He smiled at his mother through clenched teeth.

"We'll leave very soon," said Theda. "As soon as Judy scrubs the tub!"

Judy threw off her boa.

"Incroyable! Injuste!" she complained.

Doug smiled as he opened the bathroom door. "Whatever you say," he said, handing her a scrub brush and pointing to the tub. *"C'est la vie!"*

It was a pretty typical lunch hour at Beebe Bluff Middle School. Or so it seemed. Doug and Skeeter were eating lunch, while Beebe shared details of the Beautify Boogerton Heights Campaign her daddy had just launched. "It's my idea to start sprucing up our neighborhood," said Beebe. "We'll have special projects, like, we'll line the Heights with statues of me. Daddy thinks it's a great idea, and he's going to pay for everyone in the neighborhood to get one."

Just then, Doug accidentally knocked his tray off the table and watched his beet burger fly across the lunchroom.

"Face it, Funnie!" Roger shouted out in front of everyone.

Doug waited for the put-down.

"Face it, Funnie," Roger repeated. "You dropped your lunch."

Doug was confused. For as long as he had known Roger, Doug had been a pretty good sport about being the punch line to Roger's mean jokes. And he could even throw back a few zingers of his own, when he had time to think about them. But today, Roger didn't even have a joke to throw.

The lunchroom noise started up again.

"Hey, Roger, are you all right?" Skeeter asked.

"Of course, I am, you . . . uh, Skeeter," Roger replied.

But Doug wasn't convinced. Roger had called Skeeter by his name—when there were so many mean names to choose from! That just wasn't normal. Something weird was happening, and Doug was going to get to the bottom of it.

During English class, Doug paid close attention to his nemesis. The topic in Ms. Kristal's class that day was careers. Doug listened as Beebe talked about her plan to be the president of W.O.W.—Worldwide Organization of Women. She finished dramatically, "And I will retire at age twenty-five to serve humanity as a spa-tester."

Patti talked about ending world hunger while serving as chair of the Red Cross.

Skeeter mentioned something about heading up the computer division of a robot company, or maybe the robot division of a computer company.

But when Ms. Kristal turned to Roger to find out about his career plans, he was fast asleep.

The laughter in the classroom woke him up with a jolt.

"What about your career, Rip Van Roger?" Ms. Kristal teased gently.

This was easy, thought Doug. Everyone knew that Roger wanted to rule the world. Or at least own a chain of gas stations.

"Not . . . sure," he answered sleepily.

"Well, life is a journey . . ." Ms. Kristal started to say.

Doug was intrigued. Not only was Roger scoring low on his usual mean-o-meter, but he had given up the chance to talk about his favorite subject—himself. Not to mention the fact that his hair was sticking out in a million directions and his vest was on backward. Something was obviously wrong with Roger Klotz. And Doug Funnie would get to the bottom of it—in the name of a good mystery.

When class was over, Doug pulled Roger aside.

"You sure you're okay, man?" Doug asked.

Roger looked up and down the hall before answering.

"What's it to you, Funnie? The only thing wrong with me is that I'm talking to you," he said.

Hmmm, Doug thought, maybe Roger was okay, after all. That answer seemed pretty normal. For Roger.

"I'm as cool and perfect as I was yesterday," Roger announced as he walked right into his locker door. "Ouch!"

Skeeter, Patti, and Doug all stared at Roger.

Roger rubbed his nose. "All right, all

right!" he blurted out. "I'll tell you. But first, you have to promise not to go blabbing it all over the place."

The gang all agreed. They huddled close to hear what had happened to the Roger they all knew and, well, sort of liked, sometimes.

"To tell you the truth," Roger said looking behind himself anxiously, "I've been getting visits from somebody . . . well, weird."

The gang leaned in closer.

"For the past week," he whispered, "my trailer has been haunted by a ghost."

"No way, man," Skeeter said.

"Really? A ghost?" Patti asked.

Very strange, Doug thought. This case was getting interesting, and he couldn't

wait to get to the bottom of it.

"Yes, really," Roger continued. "Every night these lights flash in my window. When I get up to try and see what's going on outside, I see this floating ghost hanging around my old trailer. But when I turn my lights on, it floats away."

Skeeter sneezed and Roger jumped about a foot off the ground.

"Bless you," said Patti. "But Roger, you know there's no such thing as ghosts."

"Yeah, well, Ms. Mayonnaise, I'd like to see you say that when a ghost is floating outside *your* window!" Roger whined. "Man! I knew I shouldn't have told you guys."

But Doug wasn't convinced that a ghost was causing Roger's problem. He wondered what it could be as he jotted down Roger's story in his notebook.

Later that day, Doug and Skeeter were walking home together.

"Pretty weird about Roger's trailer, huh?" Skeeter honked.

Doug looked around to make sure no one but Skeeter was around to hear what he was about to say. "I don't think Roger's trailer is being haunted by what he says it's being haunted by," he said dramatically.

"What do you mean, Doug?" Skeeter asked.

"I just have a hunch," Doug said. "And my hunches are usually pretty good."

Skeeter agreed.

"Maybe we can get Roger to invite us over," Doug offered. "And then we can investigate."

"Sure, man," Skeeter said with a shrug. "I'm in if you are."

Doug decided he would ask Roger tomorrow at school.

"Great!" Roger told Doug the next day. Then he caught himself. "Uh . . . I don't know, Funnie," he said, checking behind Doug's back to see if anyone could hear him. "What can a couple of doofs like you do about a ghost?"

But Doug insisted, and Roger actually seemed kind of relieved when they decided Doug and Skeeter would come over after dinner.

As the sun set over Bluffington, the Funnies and Skeeter were finishing their meal. Doug could hardly sit still. He couldn't wait to find out who was responsible for scaring such a big bully. He made sure he had his detective notebook tucked into his pocket.

"You seem a little distracted, son," said Doug's dad.

"Maybe he's upset about going through life in the shadow of my artistic brilliance," Judy said. "Being average is so . . . mundane. How sad!"

Doug excused himself and Skeeter. "We're going to Roger's, Mom," he explained.

"Have a nice time at your friend's mansion, dears," said Doug's mother.

Doug and Skeeter headed over to Boogerton Heights, the most expensive part of town. Roger had moved there when his mother had come into a small

fortune. They had been able to leave their trailer and move into a neighborhood so exclusive that Beebe Bluff herself lived next door.

Actually, Doug noted, walking up to Roger's house, the Klotzes hadn't exactly left their trailer. They had just moved it to the front yard. It was sort of a lawn ornament.

Roger greeted them and they all went into the west wing of the mansion. Doug immediately started looking for clues.

"It's about time you losers got here," Roger said. "This is just about the time the ghost usually shows up."

Just then, out of the corner of his eye, Doug noticed a light shining in the window. He ran to the window and saw something moving. A billowy form was floating around the trailer, just as Roger had said. And with every move it made, a familiar smell wafted into the house.

"Aaaaaaaah!" shouted Skeeter as he hid behind a chair.

"See, man?" Roger cried. "I told you it was a ghost! Nobody could sleep through that!"

But as suddenly as it had appeared, the ghost was gone. The strange, sweet scent still haunted the room.

"I'm going to check outside," said Doug bravely.

"Fine," Roger replied. "I'll stay and make sure everything's okay here."

Doug hurried outside. He knew this

would be an excellent opportunity to search for clues. As he investigated the grounds, he noticed a flashlight lying near the trailer.

"Is anyone there?" Doug asked. He picked up the flashlight.

No response.

Doug headed for the trailer but tripped on something. Reaching down, he found his feet tangled up in a bunch of wires.

"Aw, man!" Doug said, switching on the flashlight. Then he could see the wires that had tripped him. They led to more wires tangled around a tree.

"Now, here's a clue if I've ever seen one!" Doug said to himself.

With flashlight in hand, he circled the tree and examined the wires. It didn't take

him long to realize that the wires were some sort of elaborate pulley system. For at the end of all of it hung a suspicious-looking "ghost." Taking a closer look, Doug saw that it was only a sheet. A sheet with a designer tag hanging off it. And that smell—what *was* that smell? He knew he'd smelled it before.

"That's one fancy ghost," Doug said, holding his nose. He knew he had better write all this down.

Doug went back in the house. He was about to report his findings to Skeeter when the doorbell rang.

"Ugh, not again," Roger said under his breath. "You two guys wait here. I'll be right back."

But Doug didn't wait. He followed

Roger down the hall and saw him come face-to-face with . . . an empty doorway! No one was at the door, but that mysterious smell was back.

Roger slammed the door and said, "Man! If this keeps up, I'm going to have to get rid of that trailer! Maybe then this spook will leave me alone!"

Doug thought for a moment about what Roger had said. And then he and his nose had it all figured out.

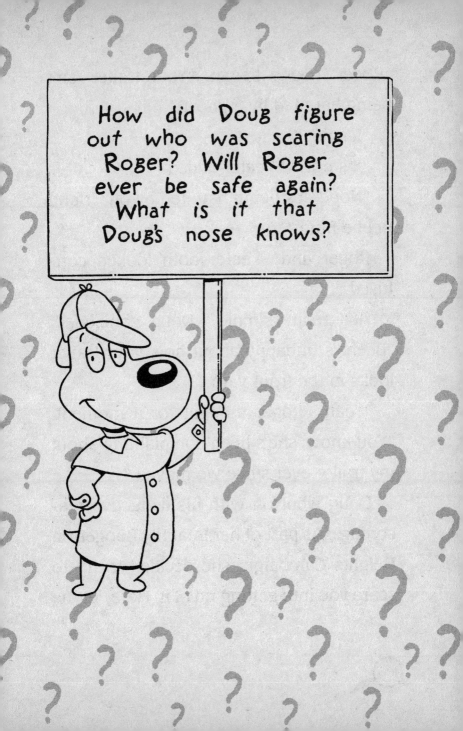

"Roger," Doug began. "Your trailer isn't being haunted by a ghost."

"It's not?"

"It's not?" Skeeter added.

"Nope. It's being haunted by our friend Beebe Bluff."

Roger and Skeeter both looked confused.

"It's really simple," Doug concluded. "Beebe's unhappy about how your trailer looks in the front yard."

"Yeah," Roger thought for a moment. "You know, she's been complaining about my trailer ever since we moved."

Doug went on with his deductive reasoning. "As part of her Beautify Boogerton Heights Campaign, she decided to try to scare you into getting rid of it. Here, let me show you clue number one, the 'ghost'!"

Doug took them outside to see Beebe's elaborately engineered "ghost" pulley system. After he demonstrated it, he plucked the sheet off the end of the wire.

"How did you know that was hers?" Skeeter asked.

"Elementary, my dear Valentine," Doug mused. "It has a designer label attached to it! And it smells like Eau de Beebe, the perfume she wears every day at school."

Skeeter looked at the pulley system. "Pretty complicated. I bet she got some Bluffco engineers to help her with this stuff."

"Just wait'll I see that little . . ." Roger was starting to get mad, just thinking about how Beebe had tricked him.

Doug said, "Hold on a minute, Roger, you've done lots of mean stuff to her, too. Besides, fighting won't solve this problem. She lives right next door! Why don't you think of a way to get along with her?"

"But she started it!" Roger protested.

"Yeah, I know, Rog," Doug reasoned. "But you knew she hated your trailer. I bet you can come up with some sort of compromise, if you try."

"Yeah, right. Like what?" Roger asked.

"Give her a call tonight and see what you can come up with. At least you'll be getting plenty of sleep tonight!"

The next day at lunch, Beebe handed out engraved invitations to a party. "It's a garden-planting party," she said. "We're going to landscape that trailer in Roger's yard."

Patti said, "What a smart idea, Beebe."

"Yeah," Roger cut in, "except that it was *my* idea! I'm a genius! That's why I'm going to rule the world," said Roger.

And everyone agreed that the real Roger Klotz was back.

Satisfy your hunger for a good mystery

Check out all of these titles for your own Doug Funnie Mystery Feast!

The Funnie Mysteries #1:
Invasion of the Judy Snatchers
(0-7868-4382-9)

DEVOUR
THEM
ALL!

The Funnie Mysteries #2:
True Graffiti
(0-7868-4383-7)

The Funnie Mysteries #4:
The Curse of Beetenkaumun
(0-7868-4410-8)

The Funnie Mysteries #3:
The Case of the Baffling Beast
(0-7868-4384-5)

The Funnie Mysteries #5:
Haunted House Hysteria
(0-7868-4411-6)